WITHDRAWN
AND
DONATED
FOR SALE

6/93

COMMUNICATION!

NEWS TRAVELS FAST

Table of Contents

COMMUNICATION!

NEWS TRAVELS FAST

Siegfried Aust ■ illustrated by Rolf Rettich

Jordan
P91.2
.A9
1991

Lerner Publications Company · Minneapolis

Getting the Message Across

Anne and Tom are neighbors. In fact, they live right next door to each other.

They enjoy talking to each other when they sit on their balconies.

One day Anne tries to talk to Tom across a busy street.

But he can't hear her because of the noisy traffic. What should they do?

Anne and her parents have moved to a big apartment building. Tom wants to talk to Anne and he goes to her building. There are many buttons and an **intercom** near the door. Anne is up in her apartment. What should Tom do?

Anne and Tom know that if you are near someone, you can talk to that person quite easily. But if you move farther away from each other, you have to shout.

If you are very far away, you can no longer hear each other, even if you yell very loudly. How do we communicate with one another over long distances?

News on Foot

About 2,500 years ago, messengers traveled on foot to take important news from one place to another. One messenger in Greece ran over 25 miles (40 kilometers) without stopping. He announced his news to the people of Athens: "We have defeated the Persians at Marathon!" —and then he fell dead! In modern times, 26-mile (42-km) races, called marathons, are held as sporting contests.

Luckily, not all messengers had to run so far. In ancient times, the news was written on a roll of paper called a scroll. Sometimes one messenger ran to a specified place where another runner was waiting to take the scroll and run the rest of the way. This way, none of the messengers got too tired, and the news traveled from place to place much faster. This was called a relay. Modern sports competitions include relay races with four runners on a team. Each runner passes a stick, called a baton, to the next runner. The baton is a reminder of the ancient scroll.

Try It Yourself!

Set up a race with one runner competing against a relay team. Who will reach the finish line faster?

Tom says, "I'm the fastest runner in my class. No one runs 220 yards (200 meters) as fast as I do!"

Anne claims, "My team has fast runners too. If we divide the 220-yard race into four parts, and each of us runs 55 yards (50 m), my team will get to the finish line first."

Messengers by Land and Air

In the late 1700s people in Great Britain began using stagecoaches to deliver mail. Four horses pulled the coach, with a postilion, or guide, riding the left front horse. Travelers also rode in the heavy coaches. It took a fairly long time for stagecoaches to take the mail from one town to the next. Mail carriers with urgent letters rushed to their destinations on horses.

Sometimes carrier pigeons were trained to deliver messages. No matter where it is, a carrier pigeon will always fly back to its home. In the past, people sometimes took a carrier pigeon along on a journey. To send a message, they attached a note to the pigeon's leg. The pigeon was then let free to fly home. Even if the pigeon was a thousand miles away, it would fly home with the note.

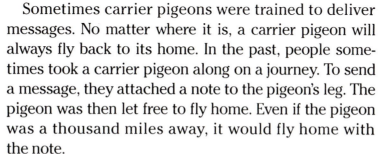

Send a Secret Message

Invent a secret code for really secret news!

Tom, for example, writes each word backward. In his secret code his name is M O T.

Anne places an extra letter between the letters of the words in her message. In her letter she has written S B E T C U R W E L T. What secret code have you thought up?

9

Signals Speak for Themselves

The signals from a lighthouse show a ship's captain the way into port. However, this ship has run aground because the rough sea has pushed it onto the rocks.

The shipwrecked people have gathered on a small island. They have started a fire to attract attention. The fire and smoke will serve as signals, saying to anyone nearby, "Help us! Rescue us!"

There are many lights that give signals.

Traffic lights tell people when to cross the street.

Drivers send messages by flashing their headlights.

Try It Yourself!

Tom stands at the window at night. Using his flashlight, he draws letters in the air with the light. Anne reads the signals.

When the sun is shining, Anne can make signals by reflecting sunlight onto a wall with a small mirror. She and Tom have worked out a code of light signals. You can make up a code yourself.

11

Flags and Gestures

At the noisy construction site, the workers can't call out to each other and be heard. Instead they give each other signs using their hands or fingers. They say: "Watch out!" "Come here!" "Too long!" "Two sacks!" "This area is closed!" "Slowly!" "Stop!" "Lower!" "To the right!" "Five boxes!" Look for all the hand signals in this picture.

Crews on different ships can communicate with each other with **semaphore**, or flag signals. Each position of a pair of flags represents a letter of the alphabet.

Using Gestures to Communicate

We can use **gestures** instead of words to say many things. Anne and Tom say: "Come here a minute," "I don't feel like it," "I know," "You're nuts," "I don't understand," "That tasted good," "I'm tired," and "good bye," just by using their hands and facial expressions.

Signals We Can Hear and See

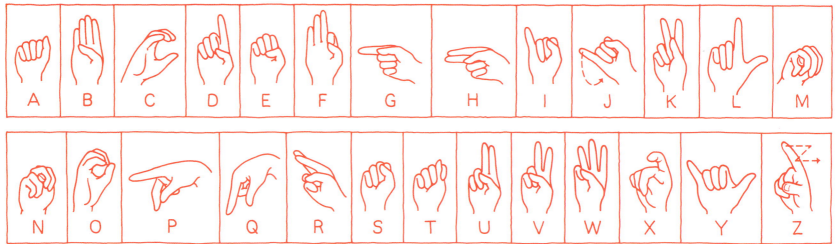

When People Cannot Hear

Some people cannot hear very well. Others can not hear sounds at all. People who are **deaf** or hearing impaired often communicate with **sign language**. There are special signs for each letter of the alphabet and signs for thousands of words. You can learn the special alphabet yourself.

Certain Sounds Send Important Messages

The toot of the foghorn says: Here comes a ship!
The car horn says: Watch out!
The bicycle bell jingles: Out of my way!
The clock strikes: It's ten o'clock!
The factory siren shrieks: Lunch break!
The school bell rings: Time for recess!

 Try It Yourself!

You can make up tapping signals to send messages. If you knock on walls or heating pipes, your friends in other rooms can hear your message. First you must make up a code. Arrange the meaning of the signals in advance. For example, three knocks could mean, "I'm going to the playground!"

The Telegraph

In the early 1800s, people discovered how to send messages using an electric current. They used a system called the **telegraph**.

With the telegraph, railway workers could tell people at the next station about train departures and arrivals.

At the post office, people could send and receive messages over the telegraph. These messages were called **telegrams**.

This is what an old telegraph machine looked like. The machine sent out electrical signals that traveled over wires to other telegraph machines in faraway towns and cities. The telegraph operator was able to send messages using a series of short and long taps called "dots" and "dashes." Each letter of the alphabet had a special dot-dash code. At the receiving telegraph, a "sounder" clicked out the incoming message and a special pen recorded the dot-dash code on paper. The code was invented by an Englishman named Samuel F. B. Morse. It is called **Morse code**.

An important Morse code message is: . . . - - - . . . It reads "SOS" and stands for "Help! We are in trouble!"

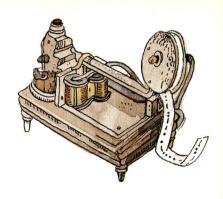

∘— a	——∘ g	—∘ n	∘∘— u	∘———— 1	—∘∘∘∘ 6
—∘∘∘ b	∘∘∘∘ h	——— o	∘∘∘— v	∘∘——— 2	—∘∘∘ 7
—∘—∘ c	∘∘ l	∘——∘ p	∘—— w	∘∘∘—— 3	———∘∘ 8
—∘∘ d	∘———∘ j	——∘— q	—∘∘— x	∘∘∘∘— 4	————∘ 9
∘ e	—∘— k	∘—∘ r	—∘—— y	∘∘∘∘∘ 5	————— 0
∘∘—∘ f	—— m	∘∘∘ s	——∘∘ z		
		— t			

Try It Yourself!

Anne and Tom are using a whistle to send a Morse code message. They give a short whistle for a dot and a longer whistle for a dash.

After every letter, Tom pauses briefly. After every word, he waits a bit longer.

Anne writes down the dots and dashes. After each pause, she makes a vertical, or upright, line to indicate the end of a letter or word. What does Tom's Morse code message say?

Write a message in Morse code letters and whistle it to a friend. Leave a short pause between each letter and a longer pause after every word.

17

The Telephone

With the **telephone**, we can speak to one another over great distances without having to learn complicated codes. The word *telephone* comes from the Greek words *tele* (far) and *phone* (sound). Alexander Graham Bell, a teacher of the deaf, invented the telephone in 1876 in Boston, Massachusetts.

Bell had help from his assistant, Thomas A. Watson. One day Watson was trying to loosen a metal disk on a telegraph machine that Bell was using for one of his experiments. Watson snapped the disk, and Bell, sitting in the next room, heard the sound of the snap clearly through the receiving end of the telegraph.

Bell discovered that the snap of the metal disk had sent vibrations called **sound waves** to the electric wires of the telegraph. The electric current carried the pattern of vibrations along the wire between the two machines. At the telegraph receiver, the electric vibrations were converted back into sound waves, and Bell heard the snap.

Modern telephones work the same way. Inside the mouthpiece there is a small metal disk called a **diaphragm**. When you talk on the phone to a friend, sound waves from your voice cause the diaphragm to vibrate. An electric current sends the pattern of vibrations along a telephone line to the receiving telephone.

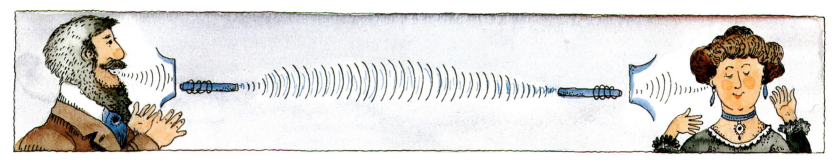

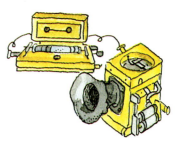

The earpiece of the receiving telephone also has a diaphragm. The diaphragm converts the electric current back into sound waves, and your friend hears your voice clearly.

In the very first telephones, the earpiece and the mouthpiece were combined. Within a few years, all telephones were made with separate ear and mouthpieces.

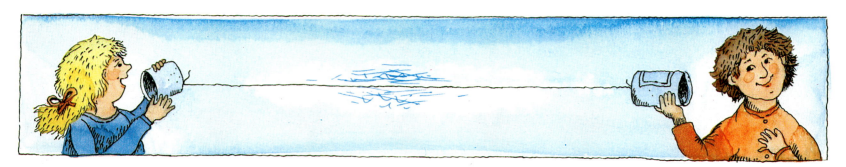

Make a Telephone

Anne and Tom are talking to each other with a homemade telephone. Their telephone system consists of two cans tied together with a string.

To make a phone system, cut the tops off of two cans and punch a hole through the bottom of each one.

Thread a string through the hole in each can and tie a knot at both ends. Stretch the string tightly.

When you speak into one tin can, vibrations travel across the string. The bottoms of the cans act like diaphragms and pass on the sound waves.

The First Telephone Calls

Miss, this is number 7 speaking. Please connect me with number 13.

Hello, this is number 13.

The first telephones did not have dials or push buttons. They had cranks. To make a phone call, you picked up the handset, or **receiver**, and turned the crank. This would connect you to a **switchboard**. The switchboard operator connected you to your friend's telephone by plugging your phone line into the jack, or hole, that was attached to your friend's phone line.

Dial, or rotary, telephones were introduced in 1896. Long-distance service within the United States began in 1915. By 1927 you could place a call across the Atlantic Ocean—from New York to London.

One moment.

This is what the first telephones looked like. The dates show the year each phone was built. Look at the variety of telephones and the way the design improved through the years.

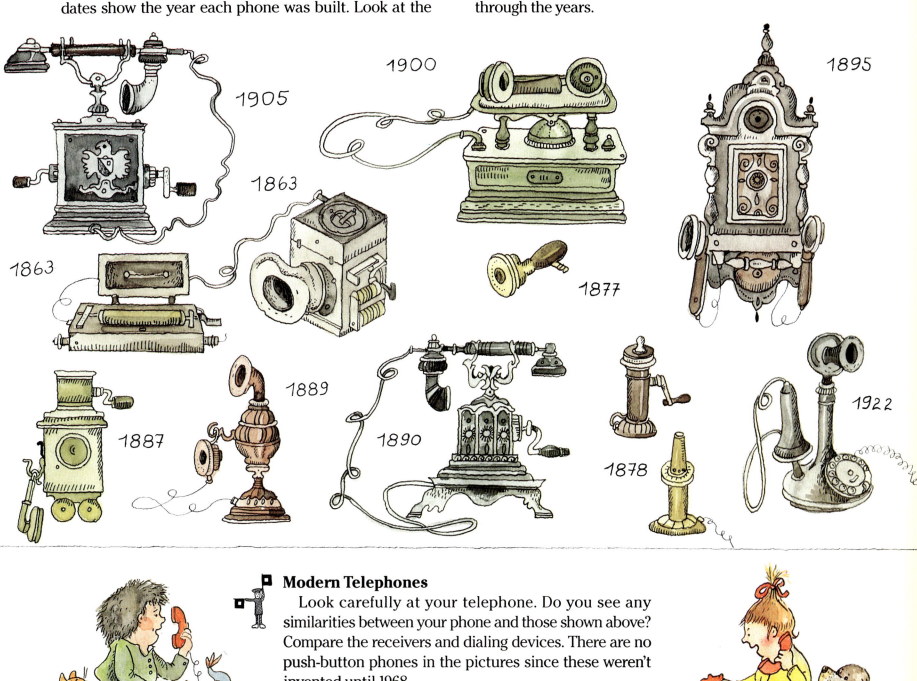

Modern Telephones

Look carefully at your telephone. Do you see any similarities between your phone and those shown above? Compare the receivers and dialing devices. There are no push-button phones in the pictures since these weren't invented until 1968.

Telephone Numbers

There are three kinds of telephone calls: local, long-distance, and international. Almost all local and long-distance telephone connections are made automatically without the help of a switchboard operator.

Every telephone line has a phone number made up of seven digits. The first three digits in your phone number indicate the area of the city or county where you live. When you call someone in your own city, you are making a local call.

If you want to call someone in a distant city or state, you must place a long-distance call. To do this, you first dial the number 1. Then you dial an **area code**, a three-digit number that indicates the area of the country you want to call.

Sometimes two cities might have the same area code even though they are many miles apart. To call long distance within your own area code, you dial the number 1 and then the seven-digit phone number.

If you want to call a foreign country, you need to dial even more numbers. Sometimes you may need the help of a phone company operator to make an international call.

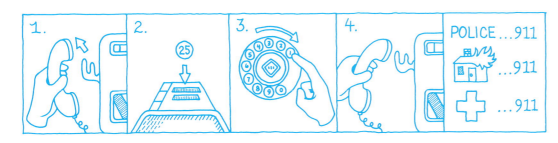

If you have an emergency, call 911.

Using a Pay Phone

For 25 cents you can call a friend from a pay phone.
1. Lift the receiver.
2. Put in your coins.
3. Dial the number.
4. Wait for an answer.

You might get a busy signal, an **answering machine**, or no answer at all.

Some pay phones operate with a special credit card instead of coins. You can often find these special phones at airports and hotels.

Making a Telephone Call

Anne looks up Tom's phone number in the telephone book. The names are in alphabetical order by last name, like words in a dictionary. Tom's last name is Wagner, so Anne looks under "W."

When Anne picks up the telephone receiver, an electric signal travels from her phone to a telephone company office. All telephones are connected to a phone company office by telephone wires.

When Anne puts her ear to the earpiece, she hears a **dial tone**. This humming sound tells her the telephone is ready for her to make a call.

Each number she dials sends an electric signal to the phone company office. There, an automatic switching system connects Anne's phone line to Tom's phone line.

The connection is made, and Tom's phone rings. He picks up the receiver and says "hello."

If Tom had not been home, the phone would have kept ringing until Anne hung up. If Tom was talking to someone else, Anne would have gotten a busy signal, which sounds like "beep, beep, beep."

As Anne talks, the diaphragm in her telephone converts the sound of her voice into patterns of electric current.

Tom can hear Anne's words because the pattern is converted back into sound waves through the diaphragm in his earpiece.

Try It Yourself!

Call a friend. Look up your friend's phone number in your city's telephone book. Maybe you keep a special book with all your friends' phone numbers.

Long-Distance Communication

People can make international calls with the help of communications **satellites** and underwater **cables**. If you live in Chicago and you dial a friend's telephone number in London, your call will first go through the phone lines to a receiving station near your house.

From there, the electric signals from your call will be converted into **radio waves**. These waves travel through the air to a communications satellite orbiting 22,000 miles (35,000 km) above the Earth.

The satellite amplifies (strengthens) the radio waves and aims them toward the appropriate receiving station in London. That station will convert the radio waves back into electric signals and send them to your friend's telephone.

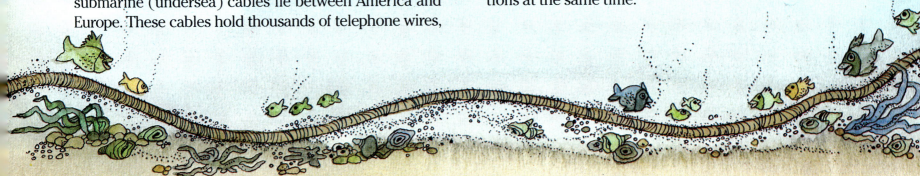

Some telephone calls travel under the ocean. Large submarine (undersea) cables lie between America and Europe. These cables hold thousands of telephone wires, and one cable can transmit more than 3,000 conversations at the same time.

Sending Written Communications

With a **teletype** machine, people can send written messages overseas in just minutes. When you type a message into a teletypewriter, electric signals travel along a telephone line to a teletypewriter at another location. The receiving teletypewriter reads the signals and prints out the message.

Newspaper reporters used teletype as early as the 1950s to send news stories quickly. In the 1980s, the teletypewriter was replaced by computers and **fax machines**.

"Fax" is short for "facsimile," which means "exact copy or likeness." When you "fax" a document, the images and letters are converted into electric signals and sent over telephone lines. A receiving fax machine decodes the signals and prints an exact likeness of the document. It usually takes less than a minute to fax a document anywhere in the world.

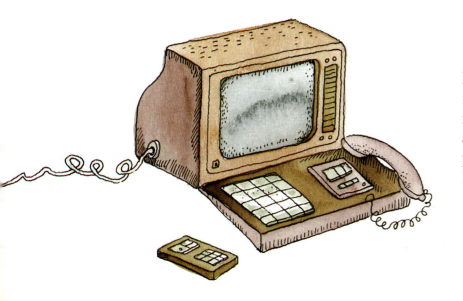

Computers are now a common tool in homes and business offices. **Modems** are machines that let you send information from your computer to another computer anywhere in the world. Modems use telephone lines to send electric signals just like fax machines do.

The Videophone

The telephone rings. Anne's mother says, "That must be Aunt Ingrid!"

But something's different about this call.

Anne's mother can see Aunt Ingrid on the television screen!

When Aunt Ingrid hangs up, the television goes back to showing the TV program.

Telephone companies have experimented with installing **videophones** in households. Some videophones use normal television screens while others use their own special monitors. Video telephone service has been available since 1970. But it takes complicated equipment to transmit pictures through the phone lines, and this has made the videophone too expensive for most people.

Cordless Telephones

Some telephones aren't connected to cables. Telephones in cars, trains, and airplanes transmit messages using radio waves. Since these telephones aren't connected to wires and cables, people can carry them wherever they go. Cordless telephones are also called **cellular phones**.

The radio waves from cellular phones can only travel short distances. Because of this, cities are broken up into areas called "cells." Each cell has a receiving station that gathers and directs the radio waves. As a person talking on a cordless phone travels from cell to cell, a computer automatically moves the radio signal to the proper receiving station without any interruption in the phone conversation.

Imagine a telephone that would let you talk to astronauts on the Moon.

Glossary

answering machine: a device that lets people leave a message if they call you by telephone and you are not home

area code: three digits before a phone number that designate the part of the country where a person lives

cable: a large group of telephone lines bound together inside a protective covering

cellular phone: a portable telephone that is not connected to telephone wires

deaf: unable to hear

dial tone: a humming sound that signals that your telephone is ready for dialing

diaphragm: a metal disk inside a telephone that vibrates when it is hit by sound waves

fax machine: a device that lets you send a copy of a document over telephone lines

gestures: body movements that express ideas or emotions

intercom: a system that allows people in different parts of a home or office to speak to one another using microphones and loudspeakers

modem: a machine that allows you to send information from one computer to another by means of the telephone lines

Morse code: a system of dots and dashes, representing letters in the alphabet, that is used to send messages over telegraph wires

radio wave: a wave of electrical energy that travels through the air

receiver: the handset of a telephone

satellite: a spacecraft that can receive and send radio signals from Earth

semaphore: a system for communicating using flag signals

sign language: a system for communicating using hand signals

sound waves: vibrations—created by things like speech, musical instruments, and objects striking one another—that travel through the air

switchboard: a station where lines from different telephones are connected to one another

telegram: a message sent along a telegraph wire

telegraph: a communication system that uses wires and electrical impulses to send messages

telephone: a system, using wires and electrical signals, that allows people to speak to one another over long distances

teletype: a device for typing messages to be sent over telephone lines

videophone: a telephone with a monitor that lets you see the person you are talking to

Author Siegfried Aust loves both technology and writing for children. Aust has combined his interests in the Fun with Technology series. He is a teacher who has written many books for young readers.

Rolf Rettich has illustrated nearly 150 books for children. In the past, Rettich preferred illustrating children's fiction. But since working on the Fun with Technology series, he enjoys nonfiction just as much.

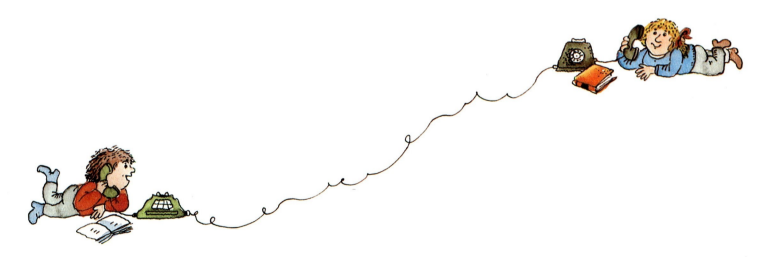

This edition first published 1991 by Lerner Publications Company. All English language rights reserved.

Translation copyright © 1991 by Lerner Publications Company. Translated from the German by Amy Gelman. Additional text and illustrations copyright © 1991 by Lerner Publications Company. Original edition copyright © 1984 by Verlag Carl Ueberreuter, Vienna, under the title Von Marathon zum Telefon: Nachrichten gehen auf die Reise.

All rights reserved. International copyright secured. No part of this book may be reproduced or transmitted in any form or by any means, electronic or mechanical, including photocopying and recording, or by any information storage or retrieval system, without permission in writing from the publisher, except for the inclusion of brief quotations in an acknowledged review.

Library of Congress Cataloging-in-Publication Data

Aust, Siegfried
    [Von Marathon zum Telefon. English]
    Communication! news travels fast / Siegfried Aust ; illustrated by Rolf Rettich.
        p.   cm.
    Summary: Explains different ways people have communicated throughout history up to the present day, including carrier pigeon, smoke signals, and fax.
    ISBN 0-8225-2153-9 (lib. bdg.)
    1. Communication—Juvenile literature. [1. Communication.] I. Rettich, Rolf, ill. II. Title.
P91.2.A9   1991
302.2—dc20   90-22348
                                                           CIP
                                                            AC

Manufactured in the United States of America

1 2 3 4 5 6 7 8 9 10 00 99 98 97 96 95 94 93 92 91